DISORDER

stop

the

bullshit

Disorder
A Political Fable

Leslie Kaplan
Translation and afterword by Jennifer Pap

Disorder: A Political Fable

© Leslie Kaplan, 2020
Translation and afterword © Jennifer Pap, 2020
This edition © 2020 AK Press (Chico, Edinburgh)

ISBN: 978-1-84935-393-9
E-ISBN: 978-1-84935-394-6
Library of Congress Control Number: 2020933424

AK Press	AK Press
370 Ryan Ave. #100	33 Tower St.
Chico, CA 95973	Edinburgh EH6 7BN
USA	Scotland
www.akpress.org	www.akuk.com
akpress@akpress.org	ak@akedin.demon.co.uk

Please contact us to request the latest AK Press distribution catalog,
which features books, pamphlets, zines, and stylish apparel published
and/or distributed by AK Press. Alternatively, visit our websites for the
complete catalog, latest news, and secure ordering.

Cover design and illustrations by T.L. Simons ~ tlsimons.com
Printed in the USA on acid-free, recycled paper
Originally published as *Désordre* by P.O.L. Editeur (Paris) in 2019

CONTENTS

Disorder

THAT SPRING SAW A SERIES OF UNUSUAL CRIMES, quickly dubbed "19th century" crimes by the press. They were committed by exploited people of all sorts, clerks, wage earners, farm workers, various kinds of household help, all kinds of people stuck in poverty, and those killed were bosses (male and female), people who thought "you just have to...," to do what? Do this or that, study, succeed, get a nice suit, make an effort, cross the street, etc. Clearly, France was divided in two, those who were for the criminals and those who were for the victims. But the fact is that the trend didn't stop, it grew and spread, almost every day brought a new incident, sometimes more than one, in the cities, in the country, something was always happening. Some of the killers managed to get away, but most were arrested and were quick to claim responsibility for their crime, they even laughed openly, mockingly, and made jokes that were not really funny, in short the world was upside down. Or rather it was a throwback to that 19th century

LESLIE KAPLAN

that was of course imaginary, but even so the class line was so clearly visible that no one could avoid thinking about it, and that's why the term "19th century crime," coined by a journalist with a column in a respectable regional newspaper, had taken hold and was heard everywhere. What no one could understand was why all these crimes were occurring simultaneously, why all at once? First in March, then in April. Had there been any warning signs? If so, no one could pin them down.

But the savage nature of the crimes was unquestionable. They weren't savage like the Papin Sisters' crime, those household maids who had killed and mutilated their mistresses, tearing out their eyes, even if one young woman being arrested had sighed, "Ah the Papin sisters..." No, these crimes weren't *like* ... but savage... yes, savage... sudden, quick, unmotivated, no, perhaps not unmotivated, but nonetheless strange, impersonal, really insane. A model employee at a bank, twenty-five years of service, who suddenly drops

2

a safe on the head of his director. A Portuguese mechanic who strangles his boss in the garage with wire that was close at hand. A chauffeur who

drives the chief executive's car into a wall (he himself jumps out before impact). Women were not to be outdone. Countless nurses were found to have poisoned their patients, so much so that it quickly became the practice for rich or even well-off people to have a family member give the shots. An employee in one butcher shop used a knife on

her boss, a trainee at another one used her apron. Everywhere, North and South, East and West, in Paris and in the provinces, in cities, towns, and rural areas, a wind of madness.

But was it madness? There were debates in newspapers, magazines, some journals: "Causality(ies) of crime," "The Reasons for Violence," "Why Hatred?" "The Origins of Murder, the Murder of Origins," nothing was very convincing. One book was all the rage, everyone read it, it was sold even in the most out of the way train stations, at least where there still was a train station, but the book's title was what made its success, *Madness and Society*, inside it was a disappointing mess with nothing on madness or society really, just clichés. A sociology professor mobilized some very enthusiastic students to conduct a survey, but they came back empty handed. *Group Psychology and the Analysis of the Ego* was read and reread, but it didn't correspond to the facts at hand. Two young philosophers, Hegelians—all that is real is rational—signed an article on "the rationality of crime," which caused a big stir, but after some intense debate, it was forgotten.

It was also observed that all these great many crimes were committed independently, there was no connection between the criminals, they didn't claim to be part of a movement and made no reference to the others. For that matter, they said little and explained themselves less. They only reported a kind of satisfaction, something like the feeling of a job well done, or in some (rare) cases of a duty fulfilled, but in an individual, even individualist, sense.

A very pretty and anorexic young woman, still almost a teenager, who worked in the cosmetics department of the Monoprix St Michel. Lipstick, foundation, mascara, creams and blush, powders and glitter. Varnish. Nail polish. She lived at Garges-lès-Gonesses with her mother and grandmother, and took the bus and the RER to get to work. Her boss, the manager of the ladies department of the store, liked her and called her "Sweetie." He was knocked down by a stool, a low one with metal legs. The newspapers quoted the words of the grandmother, who when reached on the phone, had exclaimed "Oh my goodness."

A Moroccan immigrant worker who'd lived outside Paris for fifteen years, a furnished room in the southern suburbs. He had taken evening classes for years, and went back every summer to the Casablanca neighborhood where he had been born, where his wife and six children still lived, three girls and three boys he adored. He worked at a huge construction site north of Paris, at Stains, a new complex was being built with a ten-screen theatre, and the public relations team had organized a tour of the site, television crews, local personalities. Ali, that wasn't his name but everyone called him that, had used a jackhammer and before he was stopped had killed three people.

A teacher, almost retirement age, loved by his students, respected by his director, made the mistake of arguing with the inspector from the Ministry of Education who had turned up unannounced to visit his class. A grammar point, how to form plurals of irregular nouns, it quickly turned ugly, grammar, pedagogy, how to form plurals, the inspector was smothered with a blackboard eraser.

A literature student, 21, union supporter, getting a Masters Degree. Taking the oral exam on Diderot's *Memoirs of a Nun*, two paragraphs into her analysis, she grabbed the professor seated next to her by the tie, shouted "Hands off me you dirty bastard," and strangled him on the spot.

A stocker whose grandparents had come from Senegal in the 1960s. He lived in Paris on the Boulevard Barbès near the elevated train and had worked for years in an African neighborhood supermarket, vegetables and fruit, green bananas and sweet potatoes, pineapple, manioc. He had never gotten along with the woman who was his boss and also ran the cash register, various complaints and he thought she was robbing him. One Saturday evening, with a big crowd in the store, he dropped a bag of coffee beans, one hundred fifty pounds, on her head.

The list got longer, at the end of March the media started talking about recurring incidents, by April it was undeniable that something was happening, but what? Some tried to classify the incidents. One essayist, in a well-crafted piece, analyzed each crime, first one and then another, showing that in point of fact there really was a common element shared by all of them, it was the class element, someone really had to say the word. Or a

11

refusal, one could at least venture to say, of dom-ination. He spoke of "ruthless aggressiveness," and even though the term, meaning a complete absence of guilt feelings, was well known, it made quite an impact. No clear demands were made, but there was something similar about the tone, so to speak, of the killings, or their manner, or their style. Style? When this word was used, there was an outcry, how could anyone speak of style, it was decadent, it smacked of the end of civiliza-tion, and yet still... True, there was no question of murder for profit, there was no profit to be had, and clearly no question of crimes of passion, on the contrary. The killer always had a relationship with the victim that was close and distant at the same time. He was connected, yes, but not really involved. He kept a certain distance. And any clas-sification would not only have to account for the form the crimes took, but also define the motives. Hence the much-vaunted expression "19th centu-ry crimes" that seemed so appropriate. In short, no one knew what to think.

The doorman at a top hotel in Paris, spotless uniform, cap and gold buttons. His whiskers and sideburns made him look just like Emil Jannings in *The Last Laugh*, the Murnau film from 1924—the film showed the humiliation of an old doorman downgraded to be the men's room attendant—so much so that film lovers couldn't help showing their outright sympathy for the killer. The hotel manager, an arrogant little thirty-something just out of business school, had ventured a joke about the doorman's expanding waistline. He was wiped out by a simple punch with a massive fist.

There were housekeepers, there were workers. A young postal clerk, recently hired at the 5th Arrondissement branch in Paris. He was overtaken by uncontrollable laughter when he saw the incredibly long line that looped around multiple times in front of his service window, it must be said that this branch, like many others, was no longer open except in the afternoons. When the branch manager told him to calm down he kept on roaring

with laughter, while jabbing a pair of scissors into the manager's ribs.

A young woman working at the public library in Saint Denis, who had helped design and organize a remarkable exhibit on colonialism, a subject very important to her, she said afterwards, because she herself was from the Caribbean. During the opening reception, amidst the champagne flutes and canapés, she had words with the ministerial representative (from the Overseas Ministry, the Culture Minister had not made the trip). She used a champagne bottle to the back of the neck.

At least ten farm workers, each in a completely different region of the country, ran over their bosses with a tractor. This happened in Beauce,

Brittany, the Auvergne, Poitou, the North, and the Cévennes. In Finistère, a farmhand who had worked for years on the same farm, as had his parents and grandparents, used an old broom. On a farm in the South, a woman used a cast-iron skillet, it still contained the omelet she was making.

A manager of a dairy in the Auvergne was drowned in milk, another in cream in Brittany.

All over the place, truckers coming to pick up their route assignments knocked out their bosses in the office. Some, not many, set their trucks on fire.

In a crowded lecture hall, first year of medical school, anatomy, the role and importance of the cerebellum, a student seated way in the back suddenly ran down the steps shouting: "cerebellum yourself" and stabbed the lecturer.

The film world had to show its regret for the murder, by strangulation and after the showing of a mediocre film, of one of the organizers of the Cannes Festival, by a director whose work had been rather well received, though perhaps not well enough.

A young priest in a parish near Menton who had just completed Seminary. He used the church thurible, very rare and very heavy, on his Bishop, and made the front page of all the papers, not only in the region but nationally as well, it is true that he was extremely photogenic. He refused to explain himself, which unfortunately set off a number of rumors, and most commentators emphasized that the Church really didn't need any more of *that*.

Toward mid-April, a few of the big bosses and business managers started to contact each other, consult each other, and even organize meetings. They wondered if they should call on the government to declare a state of emergency. But the question kept on recurring, what emergency? Who was really being targeted? Words like class, domination, subordination, and so on, had become outdated and cumbersome, in fact this was to a great degree because of these same bosses or company directors who controlled, as was well known, most of the newspapers and radio and television stations. What was to be done? Especially since there was no clear definition of the opposition, just a negativity, there, that was the term, no one knew who had said it first, but it caught on, it seemed adequate, apt, accurate, it took the true measure of the problem. France was going to founder, was foundering, in negativity, and it seemed that the people who had become targets were those who made the wealth and reputation of France.

But what was happening was quickly perceived by some as impossible to hold in check: if you take a good hard look, they said, if you are serious and honest, domination is everywhere, everywhere is domination. That's all there was, from the bedroom (well, yes) to the most successful and modern business firm, to quaint little companies that might be a little outdated but still thriving. And in government, and in public services, in hospitals and in schools, universities, associations.

Theories were in circulation, written or spoken, but they turned out to be wrong, even ridiculous, and in any case ineffective. There was the claim that what was happening wasn't political, that reading politics into it was stupid, distorted, and dangerous in the end. No one took the trouble to refute this opinion which, however, resurfaced again and again, and at the slightest pretext, just like a game of whack-a-mole. Someone would talk about the latest crime, and immediately add, "But it isn't political." The point was made, moreover, that the phrase, "but it isn't political," ended up seeming like a magic word, an exorcism. But it continued to be used all the time. It would be propped up by emphasizing that there was no collective, no collective dimension, merely individual acts, isolated people. A philosopher, calling on Aristotle, pointed out that man as such is a political animal, but his point found no echo. Was it a question of exemplary actions, did the killers want their crimes to serve as an example? Did they want to incite, be copied? Impossible to say, they didn't speak, didn't boast, proposed nothing. Was this disappointing? Perhaps for some. But that's the way it was.

Other people, who also claimed, in their own way, to have the long view of the situation, pointed to the need to explain to the criminals that they were mistaken, they had chosen the wrong enemies, they should take aim at the system and not at individual cases. Still others laughed in their face and shouted back at them that the general only exists in the particular, and that a system without particular cases is a theoretical fantasy.

An illustrious professor wanted to return to the term "ruthless aggressiveness," which had caught on so strongly when first proposed. He pointed out that this term, coined by a great English psychoanalyst, applied to nursing infants who, out of love, ferociously attack the maternal breast. It was crucial, he said, to remember the exact origins of "ruthless aggressiveness," so as to grasp the truly regressive nature of the behaviors in question. But his analysis didn't make many waves. Did people see other regressive aspects, cannibalism, for instance, or scatology? No, not at all, that wasn't it. Aggressiveness took place alone, it was ruthless, and the Professor's analysis achieved nothing.

A group of interdisciplinary researchers, emboldened by the story of the hotel doorman, set out to prove that for each crime there was a model taken from cinema or television and functioning unconsciously. The idea seemed very good at first, but the researchers relied principally on a few cases of prostitutes who had killed their pimps and on Japanese films that were largely unknown to mainstream filmgoers. In point of fact, the evidence was lacking, even if certain themes could be identified, and in the end this was just a return to the inadequate, tired old theory of the harmfulness of the image.

Some well-known women—actresses, lawyers—claimed, extrapolating from "bedroom cases," as they had been dubbed, that the profound meaning of the violence was a challenge to patriarchal power, that the crimes tended to be directed against men generally, and against husbands in particular. The murders they offered up as examples, a woman who had smothered her husband with a pillow, another who had stabbed hers while he slept, corresponded perfectly to their analysis. Many women agreed with their point of view and took their side, but others said no, the war of the sexes and the class war had nothing to do with each other. The question seemed to cut both ways.

The movement—granted, the term movement was not, strictly speaking, appropriate, at least it had to be used with quotation marks, there still hadn't been any claim made as to a link between the crimes,

—so the "movement" then, it grew, it spread, it expanded like a puddle, like a cloud of gas—and the month of May—well, obviously everyone had been expecting this—was explosive. What was happening, and it took some time to realize this, was a sort of increasing abstraction, the crimes were still the acts of isolated individuals, but whose relationships with the victims seemed less close, less in proximity. It was less often a direct supervisor, a boss present at the workplace or on the site. Now, someone went after the CEO. Or else it was a government minister who had never really been seen, a legislator who wasn't well known, a director of a newspaper or television station sitting in an office way down at the end of a hallway, in short, people who weren't in the public eye every day but were definitely present by their actions in daily life. In this sense, these crimes required certain kinds of knowledge, more in-depth intellectual work, and yes even, as a remarkable columnist who had followed the events from the beginning noted, a higher level of abstraction than the first crimes to occur. At the same time, the killer always bore a personal grievance, he, or she, had been personally touched by the actions of the victim, even if he hadn't been the only person affected. The first case of this type concerned a representative who had come up with the idea, and his proposal got a lot of attention, of rethinking the calculation of overtime pay, with the pretext of increasing competitiveness and incentivizing struggling businesses to hire. Two days later he was pushed under a bus by a machinist (actually he was unemployed, and might well have found work, some stressed, if the representative's proposal had been voted in). The machinist only said one thing: "Stop the bullshit." The sentence was strong, peremptory. It struck the imagination. For that matter, imaginations were all the more struck when two days later, in quite a different vein, the journalist who wrote the personals column of a widely circulating women's magazine was strangled with a boot lace by a reader. She only said one sentence, and it was the same one, "Stop the bullshit."

There was a wave. One might say a proliferation. "Stop the bullshit" was used repeatedly, everywhere. The Budget Minister died at the hand of a taxpayer in Marseille, the Minister of Agriculture was knocked out by a women who raised goats in Toulouse, a deputy of the Minister of National Education was stabbed by a math professor during a visit to a high school in Lyon, and each time, the sentence.

Was the "movement" headed toward what might be called a politicization? A fundamental debate was begun, although not always in an explicit way, that took up differently what had already been sparked by the claim that what was happening was in no way political. There were discussions, it was, so to speak, inevitable and brought about by the situation, about the nature of the political, was the sentence "Stop the bullshit" really a political sentence, at what point can a sentence be said to be political, etc? The question was asked, how much can any ordinary individual—the criminals were all just ordinary individuals—be driven by an idea, a concept, a representation, and then to what, to crime, is it really possible, it was possible since all this had taken place, but there had to be some other explanation, didn't there?

These discussions, these debates, in no way stopped the crimes from continuing, from gathering momentum, they were the main event all summer long. In the course of one week, once in July and once in August, big heat waves, and—it was quickly explained that this was a total coincidence—numerous killings of directors of psychiatric institutions in all corners of the country. Immediately the "dangerous schizophrenic" theory surfaced, or rather it resurfaced, it was always there in reserve and used recurringly by the media after having been coined so as to promote law and order by a former President of the Republic. But it was quickly seen to be ineffective, the killers weren't sick, residents of hospitals or clinics or asylums, no, not a single one, they were in each case psychiatric doctors or psychologists, some older and near retirement, others just recently finished with their university training. The most emblematic case, so to speak, was of an experienced psychiatrist, loved by his patients and committed supporter of institutional psychotherapy, who during the ritual walk in the hospital's garden shattered the skull of his department head with the branch of a tree shouting "Lobotomy, lobotomy."

There was a sort of forerunner of these crimes with psychiatric dimensions, the suicide of a police commissioner in the city of Rennes. He was a decent commissioner, mustache, talkative, everyone liked him. He put a bullet in his head. On his desk, along with the inevitable volume of Paul Claudel, there was a letter, very long and a bit wandering, in which he explained that he couldn't stand to look at himself in the mirror any more, seeing there each time a police commissioner, his head full of horrible things, and it wasn't really him. Of course there was talk of a split personality.

This suicide immediately inspired several doctoral theses at the universities at Rennes and in other places, "Division of the subject and maintaining order," *"Everyone hates the police, the lasting effects of a slogan,"* "Virility and Femininity: Police Gender and Policing Gender," and abroad, especially in the Anglo-Saxon world, it became a point of reference. The police commissioner's suicide inspired a renewal of criminology studies which had long been stalled in sterile oppositions between hereditary factors and environmental causes, and a law professor at the University in Aix-en-Provence who had recently lamented the lack of interest generated by these studies rejoiced at length at this, although a bit indecently for some, in an interview given to an important national paper in which he concluded cheerfully: "Every cloud has a silver lining."

A reputed astronomer who worked at the Paris Observatory. Stars, galaxies. The speed of light. The nearby planets, the far off stars. Distances, the expanding universe. He reported petty ongoing arguments, and he was only given administrative duties, he had no more time for research. He had swung a chair over his own head before bringing it down on the director's, and had simply said, this was seen as very poor taste, "And yet it moves."

There were sometimes errors. In the Bordeaux region a farmer knocked down an employee of the Ministry of Culture, it was of course the Ministry of Agriculture that had been the target. Realizing his mistake he just shrugged his shoulders. A journalist (regional newspaper) enjoyed coming up with "Culture, Agriculture, One Struggle, One Fight," he was fired the same day.

A specialized worker—the term actually designates the absence of any specialty—seated for thirty years at the same place on an assembly line in an automobile factory. Model factory, a lightweight construction right in the middle of the countryside, excellent factory dining hall, significant year-end bonuses, carpooling and buses. Contracts underway with several Asian and Latin American countries. During a visit of high-ranking Chinese officials, the worker left her place, picked up a wrench lying on the ground next to her, and used it on a young man in a three-piece suit that she had never seen and whom she took to be the CEO. In fact it was the interpreter, but she didn't apologize and expressed no regret.

Disorder, disorder, disorder.

The country couldn't go on this way.

In the end the guillotine was reinstated.

After it was reinstated, the first crime was the act of the President of the Republic who in a fit of omnipotence and prey to an *"irresistible impulse"* strangled his bodyguard.

Immunity was revoked.

The 21st of January was chosen as the date for the execution.

After the execution, order was immediately restored.

In fact the guillotine was abolished.

Afterword

by Jennifer Pap

Disorder imagines violence in surprising places and in surprisingly funny forms. A long succession of workers simply turn the tools of their trade against the people who hold power over their (work) lives. These violent acts are met, on the public scene, with quite frenzied attempts at explanation. This story's ironies, exaggerations, and humor free us up to get a better look at our reality and the language that is often mobilized to manipulate, hide, or distort it. Kaplan is in favor of giving a push to our accepted notions to tip them over and start fresh. She has written of her affection for other examples

of the world turned upside-down: Galileo assert-
ing, despite Church condemnation, that the earth
moves around the sun ("and yet it moves"), Charlie
Chaplin's plane flying upside down in a scene from
The Great Dictator, Jarry, Buñuel, Beckett...[1] In this
book too, assumptions wobble.

As important as the events in *Disorder* are
the words and expressions that keep surfacing
to explain *away* the ... killings. Rationalizations
that avoid the obvious reasons for the crimes
keep coming: the press calls them "19th century
crimes"—denying their logic in the present. "Class"
is a cumbersome word and won't serve as an explanation. Really these killings are not "political" but
just a case of negativity (*mauvais esprit*). Those who
have achieved something know that, in order to do
better, "you just have to..." (*il n'y a qu'à...*). Kaplan
is attentive to such clichés, and to other language
that closes off possibilities of real understanding.
She introduces a powerful sentence of resistance
in the course of this story, when first a machinist,

[1] Leslie Kaplan, "Renversement" in *Louise, elle est folle* (Paris: P.O.L.,
2011).

then other workers who kill their bosses say "Stop the bullshit" (*Ça suffit la connerie*). Troublingly honest, it strikes the narrator and public opinion so much that it is referred to as "the sentence." Has the bullshit stopped at the end of this parodic text? Can we stop it?

Disorder was (indirectly) inspired by the yellow vests (*gilets jaunes*), whose demonstrations and blockades sprang up in protest of President Emmanuel Macron's policies in November 2018. Police response at protests was violent and overly weaponized (tear gas, grenades, rubber bullets). Many demonstrators suffered head injuries and even the loss of an eye—but Macron stated that this was not "police repression."[2] Kaplan felt an urgency to write *Disorder* in the face of this kind of language that hides the political content of reality.

Pour moi, ce qui a été le moteur de l'écriture, c'était le sentiment que l'on parlait partout de

---

2 See Pauline Bock, "Emmanuel Macron's Year of Cracking Heads," *Foreign Policy,* Nov. 29, 2019, https://foreignpolicy.com/2019/11/29/ emmanuel-macrons-france-yellow-jackets-police-europe-year-of -cracking-heads/.

violence, et que la première des violences, à
savoir, la violence policière, on en parlait beau-
coup moins. La question que je me suis posée
était : « d'où vient cette violence ? ».[3]

For me, the catalyst for writing was the feeling that violence was spoken of everywhere,
and that the foremost violence, namely police
violence, was spoken of much less. The question I asked myself was "where does this
violence come from"?

One character who briefly appears in *Disorder*
may have asked himself the same question: an affa-
ble police commissioner kills himself, having been
horrified by what he sees in the mirror. But his suicide is dismissed by some as mental illness (split
personality), then picked up eagerly as a subject of
academic study that seems to be going nowhere.
There is no social recognition that he may have

---

3 Leslie Kaplan, "Nous sommes des êtres parlants, ce qui fait de
nous des êtres politiques." Interview with Marie Richeux, *Par les
temps qui courent,* May 14, 2019, www.franceculture.fr/emissions/
par-les-temps-qui-courent/leslie-kaplan. [Translations in this Afterword are mine.]

seen something real and important in the mirror. At the time of publication of this translation, this passage has a special urgency, as the murder of George Floyd has spurred protests and demands for awareness and curbing of police violence in the US and many other countries around the world.

Disorder does not replay or allude to the actions of the yellow vests, nor mention the violent police response to them. The setting certainly appears contemporary, but the play of dates gives the story a wider relevance to many situations past, present, and no doubt future. "That spring" is the open-ended marker of the first sentence. To be sure, in the next sentence, the idea that you just have to "cross the street" to get a job refers to words spoken by current French President Macron.[4] Another scandal of his presidency winks at us at the end of the book when the (hilariously

---

4 In September 2018, Macron told an unemployed man that he could "cross the street and find him a job." It's worth watching the video of this encounter. See http://www.lefigaro.fr/politique/le-scan /2018/09/16/25001-20180916ARTFIG00043-macron-a-un-jeune -chomeur-je-traverse-la-rue-je-vous-trouve-du-travail.php.

unlikely) killing of a bodyguard is mentioned: some will recognize an (upside-down) reference to the "Benalla Affair," when Macron's bodyguard, wearing a police helmet and armband, thus illegally impersonating a police officer, attacked a demonstrator in the 2018 May Day celebrations in Paris. *Disorder* also takes aim at President Nicolas Sarkozy's 2008 program to impose security measures in psychiatric hospitals when it mentions a "dangerous schizophrenic" theory that is dredged up to explain the series of crimes.[5] The reduction of services in France (post offices and train stations are mentioned in *Disorder*) is a problem that predates Macron as well. Finally, there is a leap backward when January 21 is mentioned as a very important date in the last pages: this is the date of the death by guillotine of Louis XVI. So we are even invited to consider the French Revolution along with our contemporary moment. How do they relate?

5 See Kaplan's "La folie concerne tout le monde," written in support of professionals in the psychotherapy fields who formed "39 contre la nuit sécuritaire" to protest Sarkozy's actions: http://lesliekaplan.net/folie-langage-et-societe/article/la-folie-concerne-tout-le-monde.

One of the pleasures of translating this book was in getting so close to the voice of the narrator. I imagine him (or her) in a hurry and a little flushed, because he packs so many thoughts into one sentence, only pausing the space of a comma before adding a detail or moving between contradictory views. French probably accommodates such prolific commas, and long sentences in general, better than English does, and at first I wondered if I should take the strain off the English translation by using semicolons, for instance, to add some calming points of reference. I quickly decided against this, because the rapidly paced accumulation of clichés, contradictions, and ironies are crucial to *Disorder*. It's a sampling of public discourse foundering in explanation and denial.

The narrator doesn't really take sides as he reports this public discourse. He pauses to remark on those disappearing post offices and train stations, something a leftist would notice, but he also reports, without much comment, the thoughts of those who think that words like "domination, subordination" have become "outdated and cumbersome." He doesn't feel the need to repress things, just says it all, as Kaplan said in discussion with me. Within the space of one period and quite a few commas, there are the facts (the acts!), the theories about the acts, the failure or the popularity of such analyses, the entangled rationalizations, and the tangible objects of a number of different workplaces: a jackhammer, an apron, a truck, cosmetics, the omelet still in the pan. This narrator gives us all of that, as well as a deadpan humor: he reports killings in the style of a promotional brochure for typical regional products of France ("A manager of a dairy in the Auvergne was drowned in milk, another in cream in Brittany") and slips in "What was to be done" as the business leaders' worried question, as if Lenin had never produced a similar phrase. Perhaps he appears at his most agitated in this nine-comma, two-dash sentence, as he reports a series of questions that might begin to admit to the political reality of class, only to deny it again:

The question was asked, how much can any ordinary individual—the criminals were all just ordinary individuals—be driven by an idea, a concept, a representation, and then to what, to crime, is it really possible, it was possible since all this had taken place, but there had to be some other explanation, didn't there?

Disorder invites us to stop ... and keep the questions open.

AK PRESS is small, in terms of staff and resources, but we also manage to be one of the world's most productive anarchist publishing houses. We publish close to twenty books every year, and distribute thousands of other titles published by like-minded independent presses and projects from around the globe. We're entirely worker-run and democratically managed. We operate without a corporate structure—no boss, no managers, no bullshit.

The **FRIENDS OF AK PRESS** program is a way you can directly contribute to the continued existence of AK Press, and ensure that we're able to keep publishing books like this one! Friends pay $25 a month directly into our publishing account ($30 for Canada, $35 for international), and receive a copy of every book AK PRESS publishes for the duration of their membership! Friends also receive a discount on anything they order from our website or buy at a table: 50% on AK titles, and 30% on everything else. We have a Friends of AK ebook program as well: $15 a month gets you an electronic copy of every book we publish for the duration of your membership. *You can even sponsor a very discounted membership for someone in prison.*

Email **friendsofak@akpress.org** for more info, or visit the website: **https://www.akpress.org/friends.html**.

There are always great book projects in the works—so sign up now to become a Friend of AK Press, and let the presses roll!